Introducing Russell

If you looked at Russell's school photograph, you'd think he was just like anyone else.

But there was one thing which made him quite different. It may have been his name which caused the trouble.

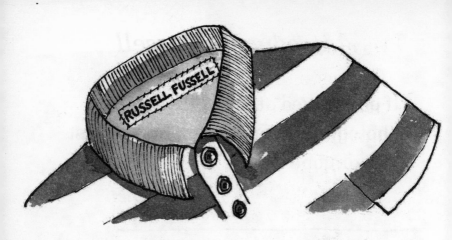

You see, if anyone spoke to him, he just couldn't help answering in rhyme.

It was very annoying.

4

He drove everyone mad.
The postman couldn't bear rhymes
coming out of the letter-box. It made
him jump.

5

Even at the doctor's, Russell couldn't stop doing it.

The greengrocer crawled under
the counter when he saw
Russell coming.

The librarians hid behind this week's special display.

Nobody could stand Russell.
Someone even said that his teacher wore ear plugs.

People tried everything to stop him, but the trouble was that Russell didn't really want to stop. He *liked* talking in rhyme.

The people who suffered most, of course, were his family.

Russell at Home

Russell lived with his mum, dad,
grandfather and big sister.
They were a happy family.
Well, they were happy when Russell
was sleeping, eating or reading a
good book.

It was when he spoke that things
went wrong.

His mum was always the first
to suffer. As soon as she called him
in the morning, there was trouble.

Mornings were not her best time.

Russell usually got held up
somehow. For example, he might be
wondering where he'd put his socks.

Just as Mum reached boiling-point,
Russell would trot into the kitchen,
smiling cheerfully.

Mum looked rather grim.

Funny how Mum could speak with
her teeth closed.

It wasn't as if Russell didn't try to be
useful. He did. He helped everyone.
But everyone ended up telling him
to shut up and go away. There was
one particularly bad day . . .

Uh-oh!

The fence needed mending.
Mum and Dad had tossed up, and
Dad had lost. Russell watched him
tackling the job. It was really
very interesting.

First the fence leaned this way.

Then it leaned that way.

Then Dad got it straight and ran
round quickly, knocking in nails.

BANG! OH! BANG! OUCH! BANG! HELP!

In a way, it was quite musical.

Dad seemed to be hitting his fingers more than the nails. Hit and hop, hit and hop. Russell felt he should do something.

Dad seemed quite unsettled, so Russell went indoors.

Indoors, Grandad was busy knitting, as usual. Grandad was fantastically good at knitting. He made wonderful, complicated things that were sold in expensive shops.

Grandad had his own workroom, full of all sorts of wool. Thick wool, thin wool, smooth wool, hairy wool. Grandad had it all neatly arranged.

Grandad was working on something very difficult, with lots of balls of wool lying in the special baskets at his feet. But when he saw Russell, he smiled and told him to come in.

Russell didn't notice that he was not alone.

Must do this tricky bit.

Then they both heard a little noise. The kitten was jumping about in the baskets. He pounced and clawed, scattering balls of wool all over the room. Grandad gasped. Russell smiled.

Although you like your baskets neat, a tangled kitten looks so sweet.

Russell, another word and I'll tangle you!

Russell hurried out into the back yard.

Russell's big sister was in the yard.
She was mad about motorbikes.
She had all the clothes and knew
how the engines worked. Today,
her big boyfriend had come round
to help her strip down her bike.

They'd just laid
        all the parts out,
                all over the yard,
                        when it started
                                to rain.

Pitter patter goes the rain.
Into the garage
and start again.

Push off,
Russell.

Even the dog suffered. Russell had
to take Paws out every day.
They often met other dogs,
and Paws liked to play with them.
This made Russell late, and he
would get quite stern.

Don't paddle with that poodle.
Don't prance with that pug.
Don't mix with that wolfhound,
or that sheepdog like a rug.

Russell upset absolutely everybody.
But there was just one person
who might be able to stop him.
Russell's headmaster.

Russell on Stage

Everyone was talking about the school play. Usually, each class did its own small play at the end of term. But this year, Mr Pumphrey, the headmaster, wanted to do something really big.

What play should they choose?

Some people wanted
The Sleeping Beauty.

Some people wanted
The Wind in the Willows.

Russell and his best friend, Tony, wanted *The Return of the Fanged Monsters from Outer Space* – but Mr Pumphrey wasn't keen.

It was Mr Pumphrey who finally
decided on *Jack and the Beanstalk*.
He said there'd be enough parts in it
for the whole school.

There were a few special parts, too,
of course.

But Mr Pumphrey had his own ideas about those.

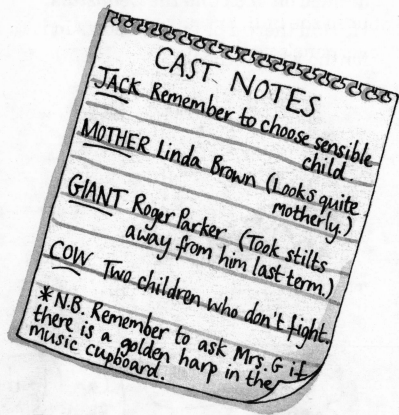

CAST NOTES

JACK Remember to choose sensible child.

MOTHER Linda Brown (Looks quite motherly.)

GIANT Roger Parker (Took stilts away from him last term.)

COW Two children who don't fight.

*N.B. Remember to ask Mrs. G if there is a golden harp in the music cupboard.

Russell and Tony wanted to be the cow, but Mr Pumphrey said he wanted them where he could see them. In the end, they were village people. They had to sing a song and cheer in the right places.

The best part was making the
beanstalk. First of all, it was laid
out in the hall, but it got in
everyone's way there.

Then Mr Pumphrey said each class could make one part, and they'd all be joined together later. Even so, it took up a lot of space.

Everything got very confused, and when the beanstalk came to be joined together, some of the joins weren't very good. That may be why the accident happened, on the night of the play.

31

Nearly
all the parents
had come, and soon
the hall was full. Russell
peeped through the curtains and
saw Mum and Dad, Grandad and
his sister. Even the big boyfriend
was there. Russell went into
a corner and practised his line.

It was more of a word than a line, really, but he wanted to do it well.

And, when the time came, he did do it well. The whole play went well, in fact, until nearly the end.

Jack had just climbed down the
beanstalk, when it began to bend.

It bent and swayed and toppled...

Help!

Jack was so surprised that he forgot his words. There was an awful silence while everyone waited.

Then Russell stepped forward.

The audience laughed and clapped.
The big boyfriend even whistled.
The girl playing Jack's mother
burst into tears because she'd lost
her place.

The giant got the giggles,
which was a problem because
he was supposed to be dead.

We shall hear
no more of him!

Tee-hee
Chortle
chortle

Behind the stage,
Mr Pumphrey
wasn't laughing.
This wasn't how
he'd planned
to finish the play.
Russell knew that

tomorrow he'd be in big trouble.

Don't Do It, Russell!

Russell was quite right. The next
day, Mr Pumphrey gave him a note
to take home. Mum read the note
and came to school.

Mr Pumphrey talked to Mum.

Mum talked to Dad.

Mum and Dad talked to Russell.

They all agreed. Something had to
be done. Russell was very sorry for
all the trouble he'd caused.

After that, he really tried. It was a
terrible struggle, and some days
he hardly spoke at all. He began to
be able to stop himself speaking in
rhyme, even if that meant saying
what he didn't mean to say . . .

There was the time at school dinner.
They had ice-cream and there were
second helpings. Russell went up
to get some more.

And the dinner lady shut the hatch.

Poor old Russell! He didn't give up.
And everyone wanted to help.
When he felt a rhyme coming, Mum
would put a table-cloth over him . . .

Grandad would throw balls of wool
at him . . .

His sister offered to tap him with
her spanner.

His friends were even kinder.
They kicked him on the ankle.
And soon his class learned to shout:

It made the teacher jump, but it
worked.

At last, Russell managed a whole hour without speaking in rhyme.

Then he managed a whole day.

'If you manage a whole week,' said Dad, 'I'll buy you a ticket for the theatre.'

SPARKLING THEATRE CO: PRESENTS:

Cinderella

TUESDAY
JULY 25

£5   TO BE RETAINED   K16   AISLE 3

That did it! Nearly everyone at school was going to see *Cinderella*. They said there was a real pony on the stage to pull Cinderella's coach. Russell just *had* to see it! He made a

GIGANTIC effort . . .

. . . and got through the whole week without rhyming!

Dad was so pleased, that he bought two theatre tickets, one for Russell and one for Tony. Russell and Tony could hardly wait for the afternoon of the play.

But when the afternoon came, and the play began, Russell wished he'd stayed at home.

The play was all in rhyme!

Russell tried not to listen, and read
the programme instead.

Cinderella

CAST

CINDERS
BARON BEEF
FAIRY GODPERSON
GHASTLIA
AWFULLIA
BUTTONS

THE CHILDREN OF THE
MRS. HEAVY SCHOOL OF DANCING

NIPPER THE PONY

There it was! There really was
going to be a pony on the stage.
Russell firmly shut his mouth
and waited.

Then, with a jingling of bells, and
pulling a glittering coach, the pony
trotted on. It was so tiny, that
Russell wanted to take it home.

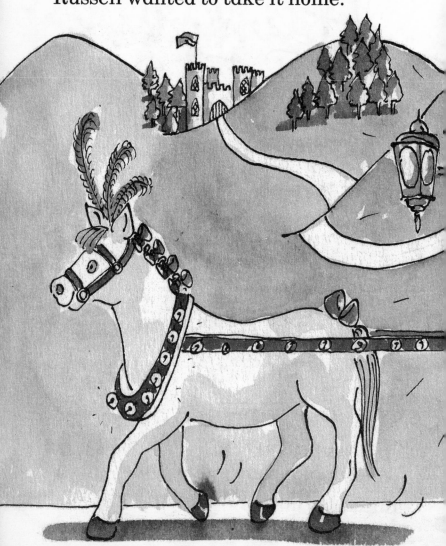

It tossed the feathers on its head,
pawed the ground and then trotted
off again, behaving perfectly.

When Russell got home, he told
Mum all about it.

We're back, Mum.
It was really true.
They had a real live pony.
I liked it best of everything
and so did my friend...
...erm...
....Anthony.

'Well done!' said Mum. 'If you can remember not to rhyme even when you're so excited, you must have won the battle. I'll write to Mr Pumphrey at once.'

The Last Day of Term

It looked as if the term was going to end well after all. On the last day, Russell took to school the letter which told Mr Pumphrey the good news. He met Tony at the corner.

Hello, Tony. Race you to the gates!

It was easy not to rhyme now. He
didn't even have to think about it.
He felt very proud of himself.

In school, Russell told Mrs Grimshaw
that he wasn't Rhyming Russell
any more. He told everybody.

Then he went to give Mr Pumphrey the letter. It took quite a long time because he stopped to tell the good news to everyone along the corridor.

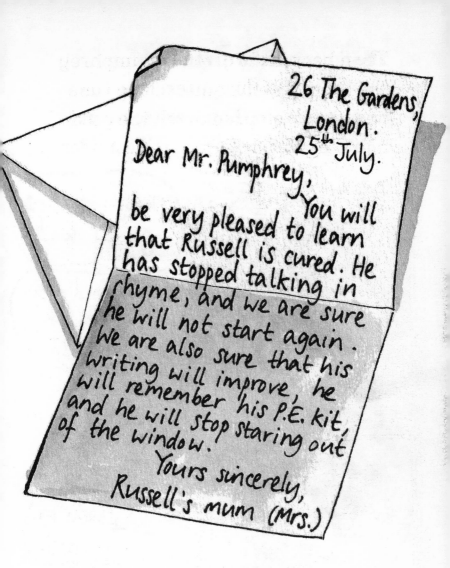

26 The Gardens,
London.
25th July.

Dear Mr. Pumphrey,
You will be very pleased to learn that Russell is cured. He has stopped talking in rhyme, and we are sure he will not start again. We are also sure that his writing will improve, he will remember his P.E. kit, and he will stop staring out of the window.
Yours sincerely,
Russell's mum (Mrs.)

'This is splendid!' beamed
Mr Pumphrey. 'I knew you could
do it if you really tried.'
It was a great day for Russell.

The day ended with the last assembly. By then, everyone was happy because they were so nearly into the holidays.

Even Mr Pumphrey wore a big smile as he read out the notices.

First of all, the Inter-school Football results. Their school had won! The captain of the team came up to the stage to collect the cup.

The cup reads: Inter-school Football Competition

Then the Inter-school Chess. They had won that, too. Mary Elliott had beaten the other player every time.

Then Mr Pumphrey smiled more than ever. He had something special to say. He asked Russell to come up on to the stage.

When Russell was standing beside him, Mr Pumphrey began to speak.

Russell, you've done really well.
It's been a struggle, I can tell.
I've brought you here to take a bow.
What's wrong? Oh help! I'm rhyming now!

Assembly was over. School was
over. Russell and Tony came out of
the gates.

And smiling cheerfully,
they walked home together
to start the holidays.